Bantam Books in the Choose Your Own Adventure ® Series
Ask your bookseller for the books you have missed

Choose Your Own Adventure Books for younger readers

MOUNTAIN SURVIVAL

BY EDWARD PACKARD

ILLUSTRATED BY LESLIE MORRILL

BANTAM BOOKS
TORONTO · NEW YORK · LONDON · SYDNEY

RL 4, IL 10 and up

MOUNTAIN SURVIVAL

A Bantam Book / January 1984

CHOOSE YOUR OWN ADVENTURE® is a registered trademark of
Bantam Books, Inc. Registered in U.S. Patent and Trademark
Office and elsewhere.

Original Conception of Edward Packard
Front cover art by Paul Granger

ISBN 0-553-23868-X

Published simultaneously in the United States and Canada

Bantam Books are published by Bantam Books, Inc. Its trademark, consisting of the words "Bantam Books" and the por-
trayal of a rooster, is Registered in U.S. Patent and Trademark
Office and in other countries. Marca Registrada. Bantam
Books, Inc., 666 Fifth Avenue, New York, New York 10103.

PRINTED IN THE UNITED STATES OF AMERICA

O   0 9 8 7 6 5 4 3 2 1

MOUNTAIN SURVIVAL

WARNING!!!

Do not read this book straight through from beginning to end! This book contains many different adventures you may have as you try to find your way out of a mountain wilderness.

Your plane has crashed in the mountains. Your only hope of survival is to find your way to a ranger station nine miles to the east. The question is, do you have the luck and skills you need to survive? You're about to find out.

From time to time as you read along, you will be asked to make a choice. Your choice may lead to success or disaster. After you make your choice, follow the instructions to see what happens to you next.

Think carefully before you act. Any move could be your last . . . or it *might* lead you out of the mountain wilderness.

You and your pilot, Jake McKay, are flying over the Canadian Rockies when the engine begins to sputter. . . .

Suddenly you're caught in a blinding snow squall.

What seemed like a beautiful spring day has turned into a wintry nightmare.

"We're going down!" Jake cries.

Turn to page 2.

Jake is able to set the plane down on a smooth grassy area just at the timberline. It hits the ground hard, bounces once, and slides into a grove of stunted pine trees. The left wing smashes against a tree, and the plane spins wildly around, then suddenly stops.

Fortunately you are not hurt—just shaken up a bit—but Jake's ankle seems to be sprained. He can't put any weight on it. To make matters worse, the radio stopped working on impact.

The two of you huddle down in your seats. Jake has wrapped his injured ankle in a red plaid scarf. "I'm afraid we were pretty far off course," he says, his eyes scanning the map. "Our only hope is for you to make it to that ranger station we saw on the way in. I'd say it's about nine miles east of here. It looked abandoned from the air, but if it's like most of the stations in this area, it's stocked with canned food and an emergency radio transmitter."

Go on to the next page.

You look over at Jake. You know he is trying to encourage you. "I'll go," you tell him. You listen carefully as he explains how to send a radio distress signal.

Jake does his best to smile. "That was just a frontal squall that hit us. Look, the sun's coming out. You'd better get going so you can reach the station before dark."

You check your backpack, which holds a light sleeping bag, a poncho, a day's supply of food, matches, and a first-aid kit. You are wearing a hooded parka, wool socks, gloves, and a good pair of hiking boots—the right clothes for a long hike.

After making sure that Jake is comfortable, you strap on your backpack, say goodbye, and start walking.

Go on to the next page.

4

You set out at a brisk pace across the high, rugged land. Since it's almost noon, the sun must be in the south. If you keep it on your right, you know you'll be headed east. Nine miles doesn't seem like a long distance. On a gentle, well-groomed trail you could easily cover it in three hours, but in these mountains it could take much longer.

Within an hour it has become cloudy again. A cold north wind has sprung up; the temperature is falling. You flip up the collar of your parka, trying to keep warm. Now, ahead of you, you see what looks like an animal trail, running north–south. Alongside it, blocking your way, is a high rock wall, too steep to climb. The shortest route around the wall would be to cross the roaring stream to your right. The stream is about ten feet wide with water boiling up in a white torrent. You can't judge its depth. Probably you can get across it by jumping from rock to rock, but one slip could put you in a lot of trouble.

The safest thing to do would be to follow the animal trail through the pine forest to your left, but that would take you in a northerly direction, possibly far out of your way.

If you decide to follow the trail to your left, turn to page 8.

If you try to cross the stream, turn to page 7.

Keeping the sun on your left, you follow the trail across a high plateau bristling with scrubby pine trees that have managed to survive in the harsh climate. On and on you trudge through the strange and beautiful landscape, until at last you see a tiny cabin ahead of you. It must be the other ranger station!

You rush into the cabin and take stock of its contents—matches, firewood, a small wood stove, plenty of food, a backpack filled with emergency gear, and a radio!

You quickly get a fire going and start heating a pot of soup. You'll soon be enjoying hot soup and biscuits with honey. Meanwhile you follow the instructions for sending distress signals on the radio. The set is of the simplest kind, designed only for one-way emergency transmission. You send out a call for help, but you can't be sure your signals are being heard.

Turn to page 10.

You walk along the raging stream, looking for a place to cross. In a little while you come to a section that is strewn with boulders. You tighten your backpack and leap from rock to rock. You're almost across when your right foot comes down on a loose rock, throwing you off balance and into the icy water. Spray flies in your face as you frantically clutch at a jammed log and then half swim, half wade to the opposite bank.

Turn to page 9.

Following the trail to your left, you head north—along the edge of the granite wall that blocks your way to the east. You go higher and higher; it's a long, exhausting climb, but it seems to be the only safe way over the mountain.

At last you reach a plateau well above the timberline. Your route east is no longer blocked, and you strike out across the high, barren terrain, glad to be headed toward the ranger station.

Though the way is clear now, you are exposed to a powerful wind. Within moments, a heavy bank of clouds sweeps across the mountain. Suddenly the squall hits you. You try to stay calm. All you can see through the driving snow is the ground beneath your feet and the blurred outline of nearby rocks. Using the wind as a compass— its direction seems to be holding steady from the north—you try to keep on course. Then you see a hollow place in the rocks, almost like a cave, a refuge from the wind and snow. Maybe you should take shelter until the weather improves. Then you remember Jake—he's counting on you to help him. It's hard to think clearly—you're so cold and miserable. You wonder whether you should keep moving in spite of the storm.

If you continue on, turn to page 12.

If you take shelter, turn to page 37.

You're soaked to the skin and shivering so hard that you can barely breathe. You try to warm up by walking, heading southeast along the base of the rock wall. If you can find a place to scale it, you can head straight east again—toward the ranger station. But your plunge in the stream has left you badly chilled. You're not sure that you can go on.

There is some brush wood and dry pine branches nearby. It might be a good idea to start a fire and dry off completely. You thought you had plenty of matches, but one pack is soaked, and the pack that stayed dry has only one match left.

Should you use your last match? Maybe it's more important to keep moving. If you take time to build a fire and warm up, you may not reach the ranger station before dark.

If you stop to build a fire, turn to page 11.

If you continue on, turn to page 14.

That night a wild storm howls outside, but you sleep well. After a good breakfast, you get on the radio and try to send more distress signals. If only you could be sure that someone was receiving them—it's hard to just wait! A map on the wall shows a road only fifteen miles farther east. But in these mountains you'd never get that far in one day. You would have to sleep outside overnight. And if you got lost, you and Jake might never make it off the mountain alive.

*If you decide to hike to the road,
turn to page 31.*

If you decide to wait for help, turn to page 59.

You gather some dry pine branches and twigs. Taking great care to shield your only match from the wind, you light the fire. It catches. Soon you have a good blaze going.

It takes a couple of hours for you to get really warm and dry. Now you must hurry. The sky has darkened, the wind is blowing stronger, and a fine, light snow is stinging your cheeks.

Continuing on a few hundred yards, you discover a trail up the rock wall—a steep mountain gully. The center line of the gully looks like the easiest way up, but you're concerned about the big rocks near the top; some of them look pretty loose. Maybe you should climb up the side of the gully, even though it's steeper and the footing less secure.

You have a vague memory of someone's saying that you shouldn't climb up the center line of a mountain gully. Or did they say you shouldn't climb up the side of a gully? You can't remember.

*If you climb up the side of the gully,
turn to page 21.*

*If you climb up the center line of the gully,
turn to page 25.*

Gritting your teeth, you struggle on. You are determined to keep moving. You manage to reach a ledge that is sheltered from the full force of the wind. From here you're going to have to climb steeply upward, up a high ridge to the top of the mountain. Climbing is hard work, but the footing is secure. The snow lets up and visibility improves. You make good progress up the long slope, climbing higher and higher until you find yourself above the clouds hanging over the valley. Everywhere you look, snow-capped peaks jut up into the crystalline sky. You have never seen such a view!

You keep climbing, but you have to breathe a lot harder now. You start to cough. Soon you have a headache and begin to feel dizzy. Yet you are quite warm from the hard work of climbing, and not in immediate danger of developing hypothermia (becoming dangerously chilled).

Should you struggle on to the top? It can't be more than three hundred feet to the crest of the ridge. Or should you retreat back down the mountain, giving up the ground you've so painfully won?

If you keep climbing, turn to page 96.

*If you go back down the mountain,
turn to page 15.*

You continue on, skirting the southeast edge of the rock wall, looking for a way up. But the cold wind penetrates your wet clothes. Your teeth chatter as you stumble on, hunched over against the cold. Your vision begins to blur, and you're getting short of breath. Your legs feel like rubber. You stumble over a rock and fall. You try to get up but lurch crazily from side to side, then sink back to the ground. You lie there in a heap, shaking, too weak to look for shelter. Dimly you realize what has happened. Your body temperature has fallen dangerously low. There's no doubt about it—you have the symptoms of advanced hypothermia: your body is losing heat faster than it can generate it. If only you had started a fire and warmed yourself. Now it is too late.

The End

Reluctantly you retrace your steps and go down the mountain. By the time you've descended about a thousand feet, you're feeling a lot better. From your present vantage point you can see a snowfield that fills a broad valley, a mile or so wide, lying between two high peaks. From the direction of the sun you decide that going east across the snowfield is probably the best route to the ranger station.

Fortunately the snow is packed hard; you won't break through the crust. Within a few hours you are able to travel halfway across the field. There's still a chance of reaching the ranger station by dark.

But the weather is becoming a problem. You know that the weather can change with frightening suddenness in the mountains. And that's what's happening now. The sun is gone. It has started to snow, and a stiff wind is blowing, stinging your cheeks and nose and clouding your eyes. You slog onward, but the storm worsens. Soon you're facing blizzard conditions.

If you push on, turn to page 63.

If you dig a snow cave and crawl inside for shelter, turn to page 22.

The moment Chauncey is free, he grabs the shotgun. "I know how to use this," he says.

Moments later Gino returns. Chauncey points the shotgun at him and backs him into the corner. While Chauncey guards Gino, you try to get the radio working. Through trial and error, you are able to make it work, and by sunset you are in touch with the Royal Canadian Mounted Police.

"Don't let your prisoner move," the Mounties tell you. "We'll have a helicopter there at dawn."

You and Chauncey exchange glances. It's going to be a long, tense night. Gino is beginning to look nervous. Maybe you should try to tie him up so he can't jump you.

If you tell Chauncey to hold the gun on Gino while you try to tie him up, turn to page 99.

If you tell Chauncey he should just watch Gino, turn to page 104.

Keeping the sun on your right, you follow the trail. It's marked from time to time by little piles of rocks. You must be nearing civilization! With any luck you'll reach the next ranger station before dark.

By noon you've descended well below the tree line. Now the trail is marked by little white markings painted on the scrubby pine trees along the way.

You're really hungry, so you perch on a rock and feast on crackers and peanut butter from your food pack. You'd like to lie back and nap for a while, but you know you've got to keep moving. The wind is picking up, the sky is darkening, and the temperature is dropping every minute.

Go on to the next page.

You hurry along. The ranger station can't be more than three or four miles away, judging by the fast progress you've made. But the sky darkens and snow begins to fly. There are scattered little flakes at first; then it begins to snow heavily. The wind howls, and the chilly blasts begin working through your parka. You're not only getting cold; you're getting scared. You open up your food pack and eat some more peanut butter. You need extra energy, extra calories. Even the peanut butter tastes cold.

Quickly you strap your pack on again and get moving. Can't waste time. The visibility is getting worse as the snow thickens. But you keep up your pace, traveling along the side of the mountain. By now you feel pretty sure that you've covered most of the distance from the last cabin. There can't be more than a mile or so to go to reach shelter—and the radio. Through the hard-driving snow, you see a rock overhang that arches around, forming what looks like a tiny cave. Should you take shelter and wait for the storm to let up, or should you keep going?

If you take shelter, turn to page 37.

If you keep going, turn to page 27.

It's a long, exhausting climb up the side of the gully. About halfway up, a huge boulder crashes down the center, scaring you out of your wits. Fortunately you are clear of its path, and in another half hour you reach the crest. You look out over the high plateau. Much of the land is wooded with dwarf pines; some of it is only barren rock with patches of snow here and there.

It is now about three o'clock. You know the ranger station lies to the east, but the sun is hidden by clouds, so you can't be sure which way east is. You think you'll be heading east if you follow the creek to your left. You've always thought you had a pretty good sense of direction, but you recall that cliffs and ridges in this area generally run north—south. Maybe you're heading east now, even though east seems to be to your left. If it is, and you follow the creek, you'll be heading north instead of east!

If you continue straight ahead, turn to page 56.

If you trust your sense of direction and follow the creek, turn to page 28.

You know you have to find shelter. You can't go far in a mountain blizzard, and even if you did, you would never be able to keep going in the right direction. Searching about, you notice a rock ledge where a deep pocket of snow has been trapped. It's your only chance to escape from the storm.

Using only your gloved hands, you begin to dig a tunnel into the snowbank. Luckily the snow is firm but not iced over, and you make good progress, slowly opening up a tunnel big enough to crawl into headfirst.

Exhausted by your efforts but grateful to be out of the driving wind and snow, you keep digging until you have widened the tunnel enough so that you can turn around and face the opening. You know you must keep an airway clear or you'll suffocate.

You need to keep up your body heat, so you eat the last of your chocolate. It helps. You're winning the battle against the cold, at least for the moment. You climb into your sleeping bag and close your eyes. While the blizzard rages through the night, you sleep fitfully, occasionally checking to make sure your airway is open.

Turn to page 24.

This brook has probably never been fished. The trout are not wary. You take off your boots and socks and wade into the brook very, very slowly, trying not to scare off the fish. You hold your poncho like a net and slowly work it under the biggest fish. You get ready to catch the trout and slip it out of the water. In a flash, it darts away. Again you try, and again. Each time the fish eludes you. If only you had a real net, this would be easy.

Turn to page 64.

By dawn the storm is over. A brilliant sun is shining on the new-fallen snow. You must be on your way, but you're not sure you have the strength to reach the ranger station, or that you can even find it.

Perhaps it would be wise to spend your energy another way—by stamping out the word *HELP* in the snow—in letters big enough to be noticed by a plane flying overhead. It would take a couple of hours and nearly all your energy to do it, but it might be the best plan.

If you stamp out the word HELP *in the snow, turn to page 49.*

If you continue on your way, turn to page 33.

You start up the center line of the gully. Once in a while you slip on the loose shale, but you make steady progress. You're about halfway to the top when you hear a thunderous sound above you. A huge gray boulder is roaring down the gully, straight at you. Bits and pieces of rock and shale fly from it, sending clouds of dust into the air.

You try to scramble up the side of the gully, but you don't have the extra few seconds you need. . . .

The End

You decide it's better to keep moving toward your goal. You quicken your pace, sure that your hike is almost over.

But the visibility worsens. The harsh wind howls around you. You can no longer see the outline of the ridge. Now there's no chance of finding your way back to the rock shelter. You've got to keep moving, if only to stay warm. On and on you struggle, your teeth clenched, your cheeks and nose freezing. Maybe there's a chance, you keep telling yourself. You can't give up!

It's hard to believe the storm could get worse, but it does. The wind whips your half-frozen nose and cheeks. Your eyes are blinded by the fiercely driven snow that attacks your face like a swarm of angry hornets. The bitter cold locks your body in its deadly grip. Exhausted, you fall—a brave victim of nature's fury.

The End

You decide that you have to trust your own sense of direction. You turn left and follow the creek. After traveling another hour, you see a ridge up ahead. You go eagerly toward it. From the top of the ridge you hope to be able to see the ranger station.

Suddenly, about forty yards away, looking right at you, is a huge bear! It's a grizzly—one of the largest, meanest, and most dangerous bears in the world. It takes a step toward you, then another, then stops and stares as if trying to decide what to do. It rears up and stands at its full height—seven feet tall! Is it about to charge?

If you stay absolutely still so as not to alarm the bear, turn to page 34.

If you run for your life, turn to page 61.

"No, Jake, you've got a bad leg. You've got to get to a doctor."

"Thanks, kid," he says. "I'll never forget this. And don't worry—they'll be back for you in a few hours."

You help Jake into a harness dangling from the helicopter. A moment later he swings into the air. You watch as he is hauled up into the cockpit. You're glad he will be saved, but you can't help thinking about yourself. It looks as if you're sort of a hero, but you may soon be a dead one.

Just as Jake disappears into the helicopter, a thick bank of fog blows up the mountain, blocking visibility. You can barely see the downed plane only a few feet away. Suddenly you hear a thud. A dark shape has landed in the snow—something that fell out of the helicopter as it zoomed away.

Turn to page 36.

You pack up your sleeping bag, two boxes of waterproof matches, a jar of honey, and some chocolate bars. Then you head east. The first day you cover about half the distance to the highway. Exhausted from the fast pace you've set, you have a quick supper of biscuits, nuts, and dried apples, eat a chocolate bar for dessert, and turn in for the night.

You are awakened at dawn by a hard, driving rain. Your sleeping bag is soaked through. You're wet and shivering, dangerously chilled. Hypothermia could set in. You must build a fire—fast. The trees around you are all young evergreens. Dry twigs and branches are scarce, but you find a few. Soon you have a small fire going, but you need wood, and plenty of it.

You can't find any sticks. You know you must find some pine boughs and heap them on your tiny fire to get a good blaze going. If only you had an ax! You rub your hands, trying to keep them warm. In those few seconds your little fire flickers out. You find more twigs and start another fire, but the same thing happens.

Now it's sleeting—hard. You realize that your luck has run out. You're too sick to go on. You're never going to make it off this mountain.

The End

You just can't bring yourself to gamble everything on stamping out a rescue signal. So you set out across the snowfield. Fortunately you're able to work your way to a rocky ridge where the snow has mostly been blown clear. You can tell by the sun that you're on the right course—headed east—and your hopes rise.

After about a mile the ridge slopes gently to the south. To the east, the mountain wall drops off so sharply you could only descend with a rope. You'll have to take the long way down the mountain slope. The wind has blown the snow into deep drifts. You do a lot of extra walking going around them.

At last you have a good view of an open slope that descends to the tree line, and you see something, about a mile away, that sends a shudder through your spine. It's the plane that brought you to this forsaken mountain. You've been traveling in a circle!

Turn to page 38.

You stand as still as a statue. A moment later, the bear drops back on all fours, shakes itself, and lumbers off. You wait a few minutes and then cautiously continue up to the top of the ridge. There, sheltered by some pine trees, is a small wooden structure. For a minute you think it might be the ranger station, but when you throw open the rickety door, you realize that it's only an abandoned trapper's cabin, empty except for a couple of old chairs and a wooden crate that must once have served as a table.

Nearby on the floor is a crumpled piece of yellow paper. You pick it up and straighten it out as flat as possible. It's a simple map of the area. It looks like this:

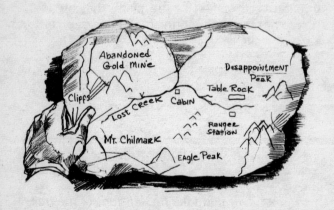

Go on to the next page.

This map is your best clue to the direction of the ranger station. You take it outside and look around. The creek you followed to get here curves to the left at the cabin. Just beyond the cabin there is a trail, which goes only a few yards and then splits into two separate trails, one to the left and the other to the right.

If you continue to follow the creek, turn to page 112.

If you take the left fork of the trail, turn to page 42.

If you take the right fork of the trail, turn to page 46.

For a moment you are afraid that the object is poor Jake—afraid that his line broke as they were hauling him aboard. But as you move closer, you see that it's a package with letters stenciled on it: Emergency Pack.

It takes you half an hour to drag the pack back to the plane, but it's well worth the trouble, for inside is a portable heater and stove, fuel, peanut butter, a tin of biscuits, cookies, dried fruit, canned tuna, soup, chocolate—everything you need. You're not sure whether you're more hungry or tired, but you're glad to see that the biggest item is a down-filled sleeping bag rated for temperatures down to thirty below zero!

While the wind roars and still another snowstorm rages outside, you cook dinner and then crawl into the fluffy sleeping bag. You're trapped in a blizzard in a mountain wilderness, but you've never felt better!

The End

You duck into the cave. What a relief to be out of the wind and snow! You grope your way deeper inside. The ground is soft. You take off a glove and feel pine needles and twigs. Getting down on your hands and knees, you sweep them into a mound. You lay out your sleeping bag on this crudely fashioned bed and wearily snuggle into it. While the storm rages outside, you sleep.

Turn to page 41.

You hate to face Jake with the news, but there's nothing to do now but go back to the plane. At least you'll have shelter tonight; but you know that the time and energy you've wasted may be fatal to both of you.

You hurry to the plane. There is no sound coming from it. Maybe Jake is asleep. Maybe he . . . but you don't want to think about it. You pull open the door of the plane. Jake is sleeping next to the radio.

"Jake, I'm sorry, but I couldn't find the ranger station."

Jake sits up with a start as you blurt out the words. A big grin lights up his face. "Hey, am I glad to see you—I've got the radio working. The case was cracked, but it works. I need to rig up the antenna. I couldn't do it without you. And there's one can of soup left. Heat it up on the stove, will you? The cold is getting to me."

In a few minutes you have the antenna rigged up and the radio working. The welcome message comes back: Help is on the way!

Go on to the next page.

That night you sleep soundly, and early the next morning you hear the sound of a helicopter overhead. But in the subarctic mountain wilderness, good luck rarely holds for long. Dark clouds have been building up in the west; the wind is rising to near gale force.

The chopper pilot radios that because of the extraordinary winds, he must lighten his load and shorten flying time. He can only take *one* of you this trip.

"You go, Jake," you say. "You've got a bad leg."

"No, kid," says Jake, "I can stand the cold better than you. Go ahead."

Should you go first and leave Jake behind? Or should you insist that he go first?

If you insist that Jake go first, turn to page 30.

If you agree to go first, turn to page 52.

You awaken to the morning light shining into your cave. The sun is bright; the wind has died down. You feel stiff and your bones ache. You are very hungry, but your spirits are high—you've survived a night in the worst weather you've ever experienced. Before you leave, you look around inside the cave. The sunshine reveals some lumpy objects that were exposed by your sweeping efforts the night before. When you look at them closely, you see that the cave served as a refuge for a mountain explorer once before. There is a moldy canvas pack, a pick and shovel, some rope, and a frayed leather pouch. Then your eyes fasten on a pile of whitened bones, and you realize that you have spent the night with a human skeleton!

Turn to page 68.

You follow the left fork of the trail along what seems to be a natural passageway between jagged peaks that rise thousands of feet on either side of you. Some of the nearby rocks glisten with yellow-and-brown specks. What is that stuff? It's gold—gold ore! You may have made a big discovery. If you can just get out alive! As you hurry along you see more of the precious ore. How can there be so much of it? Then it dawns on you: It can't be real gold you've been looking at, but only the common mineral pyrite, better known as fool's gold!

Moments later you realize you've made an even bigger mistake, for your path ahead is blocked by great rock walls that curve around on both sides. You've reached the end of the trail.

You backtrack, moving as fast as you can over the rough uphill terrain. Finally you reach the deserted cabin once again. But two precious hours of daylight have been wasted.

Now you must choose between the other two paths—the one to the left, along the creek, or the one to the right. Once again you look at the crumpled old map you found in the cabin.

If you follow the creek, turn to page 112.

If you take the right fork, turn to page 46.

Because of the season and the high latitude, darkness is still a couple of hours away. Thank goodness for that! After another half hour of walking, you come to a small cabin. For the first time you feel sure you're going to make it. And more luck: The door is unlocked. You walk in and look around inside. There's a fireplace, some matches, and, in a corner, a large pile of wood. The cabin is as cold inside as out, but a fire will soon fix that. The furniture is simple: a sturdy table, a couple of chairs, a double bunk, and a wood-burning stove with pots and pans hanging on the wall behind it. Tacked up over the table is a good-sized map of the area. There's a red arrow on it. Next to the arrow are the words "You Are Here." The logging road you've been following is clearly shown on the map. You can see where it runs into the main highway. You measure the distance against the scale shown on the map. It can't be more than a mile!

Turn to page 113.

44

Wearily you start back up the trail. You've just started to climb a rock ledge when you hear a low snarl. You look up. A mountain lion with its fangs bared is crouched on a ledge to your right, its muscles tense.

The big cat leaps. You raise your arms to protect your face. You expect its teeth to sink into your shoulder; instead everything is quiet. You lower your arms. The cat has jumped to a rock higher up. It looks down at you, flicks its tail, then bounds away. Phew!

Turn to page 47.

The path to the right is a fairly gentle one; you make good progress across a high plateau dotted with groves of stubby pines, the only trees that can survive at this high altitude. Finding that map in the abandoned cabin was a stroke of luck. Without it you would be hopelessly lost, but now you feel sure you're heading the right way.

You continue on, hour after hour. But your strength is failing. It's all you can do to put one heavy foot in front of the other. You have only one thought: to keep moving.

Turn to page 56.

As your heartbeat returns to normal, you realize that you don't have the energy to climb back up to the cabin. You're past the point of no return. You'll just have to follow this trail and hope it will lead to civilization.

The path continues to descend, taking you well below the timberline. Pine trees rise above you on either side. You're grateful for their protection from the wind, but your view is as poor as it would be in a tunnel, and the light is fading. Even in the long subarctic twilight, you must have no more than an hour of daylight left. As the creek bed descends through the thickening forest, the light fades even more quickly. You find a mossy place to make camp. Exhausted, you sleep.

Turn to page 51.

Betting everything on your plan, you begin stamping back and forth through the deep snow. Just to make the first line in the letter *H* you walk forty steps in a straight line, then go back and forth along the same line to make it wider. Once you finish the first line of the *H*, you make the crossbar the same way, by going back and forth, back and forth. It's hard work, but the exercise has warmed you up. The sun is shining brightly, and the wind has eased.

After about two hours, you've finished "HEL." But you're exhausted. The last of your food is gone. You no longer have the strength to walk.

Turn to page 101.

A brilliant sun has risen over the mountains when you awaken, rested but weak and hungry. With a heavy heart you stare at the beautiful and desolate landscape. You're about half a mile from shore on a large, mostly frozen lake. Whatever snow has fallen has melted and refrozen into a hard, rough surface. You can easily make it to the rocky shore. But beyond that in all directions lies a dense forest that leads up to forbidding mountains of rock and ice. You'll be able to keep warm in your sleeping bag, but there's not much chance of finding food, and you have no way of signaling for help. There is no chance of your climbing those mountains. All you have left is hope.

The End

During the night you are awakened by the sound of rain. Water is dripping through your roof of pine boughs. You roll over to a drier spot. The scent of the wet pine trees is sweet and fragrant. You doze off again.

When you awaken, the sun is shining. You get up, stretch, and walk over to the stream cascading down the creek bed. You cup your hands in the stream and drink. The cool, fresh water tastes good. You eat a chocolate bar for breakfast; then you're on your way.

After a while the creek joins a roaring brook, which you follow downstream. You come to a section of the brook that is partly dammed, forming a deep pool. You spot a couple of trout near the rock overhang. Suddenly you realize how hungry you are. Perhaps you could net a fish in your poncho. Should you take time to try, and risk chilling yourself by wading in the cold water?

If you continue on, turn to page 62.

If you try to catch a fish, turn to page 23.

52

"Thanks, Jake," you say. Wasting no time, you buckle yourself into the harness suspended from the helicopter. The copilot cranks a handle, pulling you toward the hovering chopper. Suddenly you see a thick bank of fog blowing up the slope of the mountain. By the time they haul you aboard, visibility is zero. The copilot shoves a pack of emergency supplies out the door. "I hope Jake can get these," he says.

The chopper shudders in the gusting wind. The engine revs and changes in pitch as the aircraft rises and flies off to the east.

You gaze out at the gray nothingness.

"We'll be lucky to get out of here," the copilot says. "Fog, gales, blizzards—the weatherman is throwing everything he has at these mountains."

"When do you think you can get back to pick up Jake?" you ask.

The pilot shakes his head. "Right now I'm just trying to get us through this soup, but this wind is incredible. I'm afraid we won't have enough fuel. I'm going to fly with the wind and hope we can reach the landing strip at Big Horn."

Turn to page 55.

You look around the cluttered cabin. Near the forward hatch is a small pack marked Signal Flares. Near the rear hatch is another pack, labeled Flashlight and Matches. Under the seat ahead of you is a storage rack marked Sleeping Bags.

The pilot is muttering something about Eagle Lake when you doze off. The next thing you know, a voice cries, "We're going down!"

You brace yourself as the chopper smashes onto ice and skids along crazily. Flames break out as the side of the craft splits open.

You have only a few seconds if you're going to get out alive—time to grab only one thing!

If you grab the signal flares, turn to page 72.

If you grab the pack with the matches and flashlight, turn to page 80.

If you grab a sleeping bag, turn to page 95.

You continue straight ahead through rocky terrain studded with clumps of stubby pine trees. You glimpse the luminous disk of the sun as the clouds thin out momentarily. That was lucky— you were beginning to veer too far to the south. You head more to the left and quicken your pace.

Suddenly you see the ranger station on a ridge up ahead. The crudely built shack at the edge of the tree line looks as beautiful as a palace to you. You run toward it, throw open the unlocked door, and look around inside.

There is a pack labeled Emergency Food, a rickety cot, an ax, and a can filled with matches— but no radio! Your eyes rest on a piece of paper taped to the wall. On it are written these words:

There is a radio in the nearest ranger station—eight miles to the south— compass bearing 180°.

Go on to the next page.

Eight miles farther! After all the walking you've done, you don't want to take another step. It's not fair, but that's the reality of the situation. You curl up on the cot, knowing that you must be on your way at dawn. You're exhausted from your trip and fall asleep instantly.

Shortly after daybreak you awaken to the sound of a roaring wind. Dark clouds are racing by overhead. The air smells cold and damp, as if snow is on the way. You open a can of soup and heat it on the tiny alcohol stove in the hut. The hot soup, along with some stale biscuits spread with a little honey, makes you feel a hundred times better.

But now you have eight miles to go over rugged, wild land. As you step outside you find a trail leading past the cabin. You know the ranger station is to the south. Should you keep the morning sun on your left, or on your right?

If you keep the sun on your left,
turn to page 5.

If you keep the sun on your right,
turn to page 18.

58

Two weeks have passed since your rescue. You're back home, laughing at a postcard from Jake. "I've decided to move to Florida," he writes, "where the highest mountain is only three hundred feet high!"

Suddenly you hear the sound of a helicopter landing—right outside your house. You run out and see Chauncey and two men stepping onto the lawn. Chauncey runs to greet you, then introduces you to his father and the chopper pilot.

"I came to thank you for rescuing my son," Mr. Van Dyne says, "and to pay you the fifty-thousand-dollar reward I offered for Chauncey's safe return."

Later, after the Van Dynes have left, you put your check for fifty thousand dollars in your top bureau drawer. You'll deposit it in the bank tomorrow.

As you think about your good fortune, you remember the leather pouch you took from the cave up on the mountain. You rolled it up in your backpack and never got around to looking inside it. You pull the backpack out of your closet. The pouch is still there. You open it and carefully lift out a tattered sheet of paper.

Turn to page 111.

The more you think about it, the more you think you'd better stay put. If the radio works, signaling your location, a rescue helicopter would probably be sent to where you are. You've got to be waiting, ready to lead the rescue team to Jake. This cabin is safe. There is plenty of firewood. You'll have no trouble keeping warm. You could live here for days with no problem, but Jake needs help right away. You keep working on the radio, hoping you are heard.

Two nights have passed. At first the weather was bad—snow, sleet, and high winds—and you were glad you stayed in the cabin. But this morning the sun rose in a cloudless sky.

You can hardly bear the thought of staying in the cabin another day. Most of all, you're worried about Jake. He must be hungry and weak. Now that you know the way, you could bring him food and make a fire to warm him. But you've learned that at this altitude the weather can change very fast. If you leave the safety of the cabin, you might never get back to the plane.

If you decide to set out for the plane, turn to page 73.

If you stay in the cabin, turn to page 105.

You run as fast as you ever have in your life! The ground is rough; you stumble. Screaming, you get back on your feet and run. But the bear is charging!

There's no chance of outrunning him. There's no place to hide. There is no chance of escape.

The End

You continue on. No use wasting energy and warmth trying to catch fish. This brook will surely lead to a road or at least a river. If you just keep heading downstream, you'll find civilization.

After six more hours of rugged hiking, you begin to lose hope. The brook twists and turns so much that you have probably covered only two or three miles. It may be more sheltered down in this valley than up on the mountain, but your view is blocked by towering pine trees.

Worse, another storm is approaching. A cold, wet rain laced with sleet is whipping your face. You've finished the last of your food and you're near the point of exhaustion. You need to build a fire.

You pull out your matches, but they're sticky and damp. When you try to strike them, they turn into mush. Painfully you stumble on, then fall to the ground. Now you are sure it's for the last time. It's all over for you.

Turn to page 66.

You push on, determined to get help for Jake. Gusts of wet snow swirl through the air. You can hardly see the ground ahead of you. You'd love to sit down and rest, but you'd never be able to get up again.

You keep moving. Your senses blur. Your brain clouds as if you were on the edge of a drugged sleep. But you are still conscious when your right foot comes down on nothing but air—air that fans your face as you plunge over a twelve-hundred-foot-high cliff.

The End

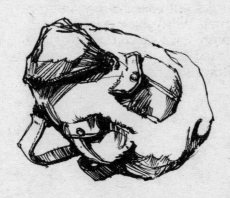

"You'll never catch a fish that way." The sound of a human voice startles you. Looking around, you see a man with a stubbly beard looking down at you from a rock on the other side of the brook. As you wade out of the water, the man jumps down from his perch.

"Nick Keegan is my name," he says, "and I'll bet I'm more surprised to see you than you are to see me. How do you happen to be here fishing in a way that will never catch any fish?"

You quickly explain about the plane crash. "How can we get help for my friend Jake?" you ask.

"We'll do the only thing we can do," Nick replies. "Follow me."

Turn to page 67.

You bury your head in your arms, too exhausted even to cry. At that moment you hear a rumbling noise. It grows louder, then fades until all is silent again.

What was that sound? Suddenly you realize it was a truck . . . on a road. The highway can't be more than one hundred yards away!

Hope fills you with new energy. In a moment you're on your feet, almost running through the forest. Then, through the trees, you see the endless concrete strip that tells you you are a survivor!

The End

As he leads you through the woods, Nick explains that he's a fur trapper and probably the only human being living within twenty miles of where you are. "You're ten miles from the nearest road," he tells you.

Once the two of you have arrived at his cabin, Nick is able to reach the Royal Canadian Mounted Police by radio.

"They're sending a helicopter with a rescue team right away," he tells you. "But the weather is getting worse—fog and snow squalls at the higher elevations. I can tell them where this cabin is, but it's up to you to tell me where your plane went down. Judging from what you've said, I'd guess it's got to be either on Broadback Mountain, which is north of us, or Mount Chilmark, to the south. Which do you say?"

You unfold the map and try to retrace your steps. Have you been traveling mostly north from where the plane crashed, or mostly south?

If you say the rescue team should search Mount Chilmark, to the south, turn to page 82.

If you advise them to search Broadback Mountain, to the north, turn to page 100.

What traveler came to this cave? you wonder. When did he come, and what happened to him? Too frightened to think more about it, you stuff the pouch into your backpack and go on your way. This good weather may not last.

You work your way along a long rock ridge, happy to find a path where the wind has blown most of the snow away. Hour after hour you travel, gradually descending to a more protected area. Groups of pine trees dot the wilderness landscape. You descend still farther; then the path rises again.

Around noon, you finally reach the crest of the ridge. From this point you can see smoke rising from a stovepipe sticking through the roof of a tumbledown cabin. It doesn't look like a ranger station, but who cares? *Someone* must be there!

Turn to page 71.

They found you! A search plane spotted your fire!

When the helicopter landed at your lonely campsite, you used your last bit of strength to climb into it. Then you collapsed, and only now have you regained consciousness. You are in a hospital room; a doctor and a nurse are standing nearby, smiling down at you.

Then a dark thought flashes through your mind. "Did they find Jake?" you ask.

"You can come in now, sir," the doctor calls to someone out in the hall. A moment later a man on crutches hobbles into your room. It's Jake, with one leg in a cast but a grin on his face almost as wide as yours!

The End

You hurry across the new-fallen snow toward the cabin. The first thing you see when you look through the window is a table near the door; it's covered with bread, cheese, sandwiches, fruit, nuts, and chocolate! Then you see something that chills you even more than the cold you've endured: a boy, a year or so younger than you, tied to a chair. His head is tilted to one side as if he were asleep. On the other side of the cabin is a burly man with the meanest face you've ever seen. He seems to be asleep, too, and you begin to hope that he is. Right next to him, leaning against the wall, are a hunting knife with a long blade and a double-barreled shotgun.

The cabin door is open a crack. You pause at the door, wondering what to do. You need food, and the boy seems to be in a lot of trouble. On the other hand, you've got to get help for Jake, and you don't think you're going to get it here.

If you continue on your way, turn to page 83.

If you decide to slip in, grab some food, and run, turn to page 88.

If you try to grab the gun and knife, turn to page 89.

You grab the flares and jump out onto the icy surface. There is an explosion behind you. You look back in time to see the fiery remains of the helicopter sink through a hole in the ice. The chopper drops out of sight, carrying the two crew members along with it. You are alone in utter darkness. The suddenness, the horror of it, sends shivers through your spine. You feel as if the furies of doom have been loosed upon the earth, and there is no more hope for you than for the two brave pilots now entombed at the bottom of the lake.

But you have no time to mourn. You must think of your own survival. At least you're off the mountain. The temperature here is above freezing. Maybe you can make it through the night. But then what? You have no idea how far the helicopter traveled before it went down. You have a compass, but you don't know which way to go. The ice is not thick—the helicopter cracked it instantly. You'll have to be careful.

Turn to page 76.

You pack up as much food and supplies as you can carry and begin to retrace your steps to the plane. Fortunately the weather holds. You're rested and have plenty of food. You know the way, and you have surprising energy. In the few days you've been in this mountain wilderness, you've grown used to the high altitude; you've become leaner, tougher, and smarter.

The sun has set and darkness is creeping up the valley when you reach the plane. Jake is in bad shape—cold, shivering, and weak. You can tell that his leg is hurting more than he'll admit. But in a few minutes you have a good fire going outside the plane. It radiates warmth into the cockpit.

Soon you have hot soup ready. As Jake sips it, he grins and says, "I don't know if I would have made it through the night if you hadn't come back."

Turn to page 75.

You drink your soup and look at the moon rising over the mountain. You're thankful that you and Jake are safe for the moment, but the two of you are still marooned.

When no help comes the next day, you begin to worry. By mid-afternoon of the second day, you are sure that you and Jake will never be rescued. Then an airplane swoops out of the sky, dipping its wings. You and Jake let out a whoop of joy!

The next morning a helicopter sets down and lifts the two of you off the mountain.

The pilot shakes your hand as you climb aboard the chopper. "You've got what it takes," he says.

The End

As you stand there trying to think, the full moon breaks through the clouds. The lake seems vast, but you can't be more than a half mile from shore, and the ice appears to be solid all the way. But then what? The moon's cold, pale light is reflected in the icy mountains around you. You open your box of flares and read these words: To Fire—Hold Upright at Arm's Length and Pull Pin.

Suppose I fire a flare, you wonder. Who would ever see it? You walk very cautiously toward the shore. Before you've covered half the distance, the moon disappears behind a mountain, and you are left in darkness. A wave of fear sweeps over you. In the day or two in which you could stay alive in this climate, you could never climb over those glacier-strewn mountains. You're trapped.

Turn to page 79.

You start talking to Gino the moment he comes back. You don't feel friendly, but you act friendly, saying everything you can to win Gino's confidence. You find out that he's almost as scared as you and Chauncey are—scared that the police will swoop in, scared that his partner will take off with the million dollars, and, most of all, scared of the idea of killing you.

"I don't have a million dollars, but I wish I could help you," you say. "About all I could offer you is my bike. . . ."

Gino smiles grimly. "Wouldn't do me much good, I'm afraid. I'm going to need a space shuttle to get away from all the cops that will be after me . . . and I guess I'm going to have to forget about my half-million share."

The pink glow that filled the cabin has faded; the sun has set. Gino fingers the shotgun. He stands up and looks at you for a long time; then he looks at Chauncey. Suddenly he raises the gun and swings it around.

Turn to page 84.

You try to think clearly. The flares . . . dawn will be breaking soon . . . they will be of little use once daylight comes. You take one of the flares out of the box, hold it upright at arm's length, and pull the pin. Nothing happens. A dud. You try the same thing with another flare. Again nothing happens. Who made these flares? you wonder. Only two left. You hold out one of them. *Whoosh!* The rocket flies out of your hands toward the sky, sending a brilliant red flare high above you. As the flare contracts, fades, and disappears, you see another light—it's a plane, swooping toward you!

Another flare bursts—dropped from the plane. The helicopter pilot must have sent out a Mayday signal and given his position before he went down. If it hadn't been for your flare, the rescue plane might have flown past the lake.

You fire your remaining flare. As it dies, you notice other lights—stars! Tomorrow will be a beautiful day. They'll have you off this lake by morning; then you can help them find Jake!

The End

You grab the waterproof pack containing the matches and flashlight and dive through the door, out onto the frozen surface of the lake. Seconds later, the helicopter explodes in a fiery convulsion that breaks the rotten spring ice. A few seconds afterward it plunges toward the bottom of the lake. You shine the flashlight on the hole in the ice and say a prayer for the brave pilots who gave their lives to save you.

You set out for the shore, shining your flashlight ahead of you. The chopper crashed only a half mile from shore, and it doesn't take long to reach a rocky ledge jutting out into the lake. The air is chilly, but at least it's above freezing. Nevertheless, you are lost in a remote wilderness.

But what's that noise overhead? Is that the light of a plane? Gone. If it was a plane, it flew past. Maybe it will be back. Maybe.

Go on to the next page.

As you reach the edge of the lake, the sky is growing light in the east. You begin to see the world around you. Pine trees surround the lake and stretch partway up the mountain slopes, where they are replaced by shale and rock and ice. Along the shore of the lake you can find dry pine branches and sticks. By dawn, you have a good fire going on the rock ledge, thanks to the matches. You have only melted snow for water, and no food, but there is plenty of wood. You resolve to keep the fire going until you're spotted from the air.

Three days and three nights pass, yet no help comes. Your only consolation is the endless supply of wood. The fire not only keeps you warm and dry but helps to keep your spirits up.

But why doesn't help come? Have they written you off as lost, or decided you could never have survived in this subarctic wilderness? You feel yourself growing weaker day by day. Soon you will no longer have the strength to keep the fire going. Then it will be all over.

Turn to page 69.

"I feel pretty sure I've been traveling north, from Chilmark Mountain," you say.

"Okay," Nick replies. "Let's hope you're right!"

Nick gets back on the radio and gives instructions while you wait nervously. Then he turns around and looks at you intently. "I reckon you could use something to eat—maybe some soup and venison and some raisin bread. That's about all I've got."

The simple meal tastes very good, but you feel anxious. The sky has darkened; it's beginning to snow. Nick sits down by the fire and takes out a deck of cards. "Do you play gin rummy?" he asks.

"Sure," you say. The two of you play gin rummy on a table made of a barrel with a plank on top. You have good luck, but your heart isn't in the game.

Suddenly the radio crackles. Nick leaps up and puts on the headphones. Moments later, he is smiling broadly.

"They found your friend Jake and got him aboard the helicopter just before a blizzard began. They say he's going to be okay."

"Thanks, Nick. You really saved the day."

"You did all right yourself, kid," he replies.

The End

You wish you could help the boy, but you are too tired, hungry, and weak to take on a huge armed man. You decide that the best thing you can do for the boy—as well as for Jake—is get back to civilization as quickly as possible.

You hurry along the trail. The pine trees along the way grow taller and thicker as the trail descends. You can't believe that a criminal would take a hostage very far into this wilderness. Surely there must be a road nearby. If only you had a map! You have no idea where you are, and to make matters worse, the temperature has begun to drop sharply. Yet you feel sure that if you just keep working your way toward the valley, you'll eventually come to a road.

At last you reach a partly frozen brook. It shouldn't be any problem—the water can't be more than a foot or so deep, and you can easily hop from rock to rock.

But you fail to realize how much strength you've lost. Cold and hunger have dulled your senses. You slip, and your left foot plunges into the icy water. In a second or two, you scramble out of the water, but your left foot is soaking wet.

You have no matches left to start a fire, and it's getting colder every minute. You keep looking for a road, walking as fast as you can, but within half an hour your left foot has become completely numb.

Turn to page 109.

You hunch over and hide your face in your arms. A blast deafens you; but you're still alive! Was that Chauncey? Are you next? You double over, shaking.

The door slams and you open your eyes. Chauncey is staring at you open-mouthed. The radio has been smashed to pieces by the shotgun blast, and Gino is gone!

"He was too decent to kill us," Chauncey says. "He just wanted to make sure we didn't radio for help. Maybe he'll get away—there's a full moon tonight."

For a moment you almost hope he does.

The End

You run for your life. Jogging through the pine forest, keeping the sun on your right, you head east. The land descends steeply. Within ten minutes or so you're below the snow line. Now you'll be harder to track. Far below, you can see a tiny ribbon of concrete—the highway! You let out a whoop of joy and run down the path, then slow your pace as you realize that if you trip and sprain your ankle, you'll be in trouble again.

Another half hour is all it takes to reach the highway; then you wait impatiently until you're able to flag down a car. Fortunately there's a lumber camp only ten miles down the road, where you quickly telephone the police. You're relieved to be safe, but you won't rest easy until you hear that both Jake and that poor kid are safe, too.

The End

88

You tiptoe inside the cabin. As you reach for a sandwich, a deep voice behind you says, "You can put that back, and then get your hands up!"

Somehow you awakened the heavyset man. He is holding a shotgun aimed at your head. Before you know it, he's tied your hands and shoved you down next to the boy's chair.

"What's going on?" you whisper to the boy.

"Shut up!" the man yells. He makes little circles in the air with the muzzle of his gun.

Turn to page 91.

Slowly, silently, hardly daring to breathe, you push the door open just wide enough to slip through. It creaks, and the man in the chair gives a start, as if he's about to wake up. Then he sinks back, still snoring, and you take a deep breath.

The boy tied to the other chair is watching you intently. You put a finger to your lips to warn him to be quiet; then you tiptoe past the sleeping man. You pick up the shotgun and the knife, then edge over to the boy. With quick, careful strokes, you cut the ropes binding him to the chair.

The boy whispers, "There's a road below the ridge, not too far away. Careful, that thing's loaded!"

Awakened by the noise, the big man leaps from his chair. You try to swing the gun around, but the man lunges at you. He wrenches the gun out of your hands and sends you sprawling across the floor. Out of the corner of your eye you see the boy rush out the door.

"Don't hurt me," you cry, trying to keep the man distracted.

"Stand in that corner and keep your hands up!" he shouts. Then, looking around, he yells, "Hey, where did that little devil go?"

Turn to page 93.

An hour later, when the man goes outside to gather firewood, you and the boy have a chance to talk.

"I'm Chauncey Van Dyne," the boys says. "My family is very rich. That's why I'm here. Two men kidnapped me from one of our hunting lodges, about twenty miles from here, at Elk Falls. The other man is trying to collect a ransom—a million dollars—from my dad. This man—his name is Gino—says that unless he gets a radio message from his partner by sundown telling him he has collected the money, he's going to shoot me; and I guess he'll shoot you, too."

"Can your dad pay a million dollars?" you ask.

"Oh, sure, that's no problem," Chauncey says. "I'm just afraid that Gino's partner won't keep his end of the deal. Once he gets the money, he may not wait around to radio Gino."

Go on to the next page.

"Do you have any ideas about what we could do?" you ask, but Chauncey can't answer because at that moment Gino kicks the door open and staggers in with an armful of wood.

You sit quietly, trying to think of something to do. You start to sweat. Time passes. The sun drops lower in the sky. Finally Gino steps outside again. Meanwhile you've had a couple of ideas. They both seem like long shots, but you're desperate. You could try to pick up Gino's knife with your teeth and cut the ropes tying your hands. Or you could try to reason with Gino, perhaps even make friends with him, so that he won't hurt you and Chauncey.

If you try to pick up the knife, turn to page 94.

If you decide to talk to Gino when he returns, turn to page 77.

With the shotgun in one hand and the knife in the other, he darts out the door. You look around the cabin. There's a label pasted on the radio. The bold red letters on the label read: Emergency Transmission Instructions.

You read the instructions quickly. Within seconds you have activated the emergency homing signal, which automatically gives your bearing to anyone who is monitoring the frequency.

Do you have time to escape before the man gets back? The boy said there was a road not too far away; it must be farther down the mountain. But the man might follow you, or you might get lost. You look out the door at the tracks in the snow. Neither the man nor the boy is visible. Even if he knows where he's going, that kid can't get very far. . . .

If you decide to run for it, turn to page 87.

If you decide to stay in the cabin, turn to page 102.

It's now or never! You roll across the floor, seize the knife handle in your teeth, sit up, and start to cut the rope binding your wrists together. You can't get much pressure on the knife. You're worried that you'll break some teeth as you bite on it. But the knife is sharp as a razor. In a few seconds you've cut through. You've also cut your arm. It hurts, and blood is trickling down your arm, but you hardly notice. You quickly cut through the ropes binding your legs and then cut Chauncey's ropes.

Turn to page 16.

You grab the sleeping bag and jump out onto the frozen lake. Seconds later the helicopter explodes with enough force to break through the ice. You watch in horror as the frigid water quenches the flames and swallows the chopper into its black depths, taking two good men along with it and leaving you alone in a bleak, dark world.

You can't see, and you don't dare set out across the ice until dawn. You crawl into the sleeping bag and fall into a fitful sleep.

Turn to page 50.

You keep climbing, but your symptoms worsen. You have to stop again and again to cough or catch your breath. You continue to climb, one heavy foot in front of the other—your mind too dulled to think of anything else. Suddenly you stop and gasp for air, but no air comes. You feel as if you are suffocating, and in a sense you are: from a pulmonary edema, a high-altitude sickness—caused by lack of oxygen—that can be fatal. This time it is. . . .

The End

You try to tie up Gino, but in a flash he whips you around, snarling like an enraged animal. He lunges at Chauncey and grabs the shotgun. You start toward the door, but out of the corner of your eye you see Gino bringing the butt of the gun down on your skull—the last thing you'll ever see.

The End

"I can't be sure," you say, "but I think I've been heading mostly south, so the plane must have crashed up on Broadback Mountain, to the north."

"Okay," Nick says, "I'll tell them to try that way first." He snaps on his radio headphones and gets the message through to the Mounted Police.

There is nothing more you can do. The two of you play gin rummy for an hour, but your heart isn't in the game. Finally you quit and stare out the window at the steadily falling snow.

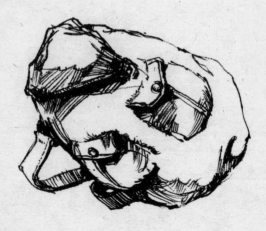

Turn to page 106.

You sit down on your pack to rest. A fresh wind has sprung up. The sun has disappeared behind a cloud. It's getting colder. You wonder whether you'll make it through the day. You close your eyes and rest your head on your folded arms. Then you hear a sound overhead—a plane!

You leap to your feet, yelling and waving. The plane dips its wings, circles, and flies off. You're still in danger, but you've never been so happy in your life. A helicopter will soon be on the way to pick you up. Your message in the snow has saved you.

The End

The odds of your making it to the highway seem pretty slim. There's too much danger that the man with the gun will shoot at you.

You wait nervously. Soon you see the man returning, shoving the boy ahead of him. You've got to admire that kid. He made a nice try.

A thought flashes through your mind. You switch off the radio—better not let the man know you've been using it. You slump in a corner, put your head in your arms, and pretend to cry.

"Stop bawling," the man yells at you as he shoves the boy in ahead of him. He ties the two of you back to back. The ropes are painfully tight; you begin to worry about your circulation.

About an hour later you hear a loud noise overhead. The man looks outside. You hear him cursing. Then, through the open door, you see him run into the woods. The noise grows louder. A helicopter is landing outside the cabin!

Moments later two policemen storm inside. You've been saved, and so has the boy. And now that a helicopter is here, you can guide the police to Jake.

The End

Chauncey has the shotgun aimed at Gino, but you're beginning to feel uncomfortable. Gino is glaring at you; his fists are clenched. You're sure he's planning something.

"Look," you whisper to Chauncey, "he's getting panicky. If we take our eyes off him, even for a second, he could grab this gun in one flying leap. I'll watch; you rest for an hour. Then I'll rest, and you guard him for an hour. It's going to have to be that way until help comes."

Chauncey nods in agreement and hands you the gun. He seems like a tough kid, but he's younger than you. You don't like the thought of taking a nap while he stands guard.

By the time an hour has passed, your eyes ache. You'd like to close them for a few seconds, but you don't dare. Chauncey is sound asleep.

If you wake up Chauncey and let him stand guard, turn to page 110.

If you decide it's safer to stand guard yourself, turn to page 107.

You want to help Jake, but you feel lucky to have made it to this cabin. No use pushing your luck trying to get back to the plane.

As the long hours pass, you keep the fire burning and fiddle with the radio, waiting for help. A whole week passes before anyone comes. By the time a helicopter finally lands near the cabin, your food supply is almost used up.

"Have you picked up my friend?" you ask the pilot as he steps out of the chopper.

He stares at you a moment, as if he hasn't heard, then nods his head. "We picked him up. We dropped supplies, but he didn't have the strength to find them in the snow. We only wish we could have reached him a few days sooner."

You don't answer—it's all you can do to fight back the tears.

The End

At last a message comes through. Nick throws his headphones down on the table. "The Mounties had to call off their search," he says. "They pretty much combed Broadback Mountain without finding a trace of a plane wreck. They were going to check out Mount Chilmark, but by then they were running into blizzard conditions. They say it may be a couple of days before it lets up enough for them to go back in there. Vicious winds in those mountains, you know."

Your heart sinks. You must have given the wrong directions. You feel certain that Jake won't make it.

The End

You decide to let Chauncey sleep. You stare at Gino, who finally seems calmer. It looks as if he's catching up on *his* sleep. The night seems endless. If only morning would come! Your head nods, and you jerk it up as you realize you were beginning to doze. That was a close call. You'll be more careful from now on.

And you are more careful, for an hour or so. But eventually the need for sleep overpowers you. You don't hear the man stealing across the room, carefully lifting the gun out of your lap, and pulling the trigger.

The End

It seems best to thaw out your foot before walking any farther, so you get a good fire going, then take your boots off and sit down in front of it, legs stretched out, to warm your feet.

The heat feels good for a minute or so; then your injured foot begins to hurt. You back away so it won't be heated too rapidly, but now it's hurting even more.

Hopping on one foot, you pile more wood on the fire and then sit at the far end of the cabin so that your foot will not be heated more than the rest of your body. You prop your foot up on a pillow. That helps a little, but soon your foot begins to hurt even more. It's thawing out, but the pain is worse—it's becoming unbearable!

You hop to the cabin door and throw it open to let cool air in. But now you can't bear to put any weight at all on your left foot. Although you have a warm shelter, you are in serious trouble—you can no longer walk! You might not be rescued for days, and in the meanwhile, what about your foot? Gangrene could set in. Maybe it will have to be amputated. These grisly thoughts run through your mind during the long hours that follow, while you wait for help.

The End

You lose track of time as you make your way along a ridge that slopes down toward a valley and seems to be a safe route off the mountain. You haven't been able to feel your left foot for a long time. Maybe you should have tried to dry it off after you got it wet. Now you are afraid it's frozen.

You keep moving; your view is blocked by pine trees, but at last you find a wide trail. In fact, you've stumbled onto an old logging road. Your spirits rise as you realize that this road must lead to a larger road, and eventually to civilization!

Turn to page 43.

You wake up Chauncey. Throughout the night, you take turns standing guard, changing places every hour. When morning comes, Gino is still huddled in the corner. Chauncey opens a can of tuna and shoves a plate of tuna and bread across the floor to your prisoner. For a second you think Gino is going to lunge at you instead of taking his breakfast. You level the shotgun right at him. Suddenly Chauncey shrieks, "Yippee!" You're so excited that it's hard to keep the gun level as you hear the whirring racket made by a helicopter landing outside the cabin.

Turn to page 58.

To Whoever Finds This Letter

As I write this, I have not long to live. I broke
my leg while searching for the gold that, ac-
cording to Indian legend, lies in this cave. I
found what may be one of the richest veins
of gold ore in the world, but all for nothing.
No one knows I am here, so I shall never
leave this cave alive. I own the deed to this
land, and I hereby will to you who have
found this cave all this gold and this poor
pile of bones that once was the undersigned,

Horace Witherbee
Vancouver, British Columbia

At first you're thrilled about finding this
letter. Good luck piled upon good luck!
Then you think about the poor man who
wrote it—how, in his eagerness to find gold,
he lost his life. Greed can be dangerous, it
seems. Maybe it's not a good idea to go after
the gold; the thought of returning to that
cave gives you the chills. You've got plenty
of time to think about it, and meanwhile
you've got fifty thousand dollars. You might
just go out and buy a new stereo, or even
buy Jake a new airplane.

The End

112

The creek winds along a gentle slope, but you have to make your way around large boulders. Jagged peaks rise on either side. Then your path descends steeply. At times you have to face the rocks as you climb down, holding on with your hands and feet. At least you're more sheltered from the wind—and you know that the air will be warmer when you reach a lower altitude. But the farther you go, the less confident you feel that you're headed toward the ranger station. Finally you realize that you took the wrong trail.

Turn to page 44.

But you're still worried about your foot. You sit down and take off your left boot. You touch your foot gently in several places, then press each of your toes firmly. There's no feeling at all. Your toes and the front part of your foot look grayish white. There doesn't seem to be any doubt about it—at least half your foot is frozen!

You slip your numb left foot back into your boot. It would take only about a half hour to reach the highway. You know there will be cars and trucks on a big road like that—someone to rescue you. But you feel so tired and weak. You could build a fire and warm your foot. Walking would be easier if you had your strength back.

If you build a fire in order to thaw out your foot, turn to page 108.

If you set out for the highway right away, go on to the next page.

You walk down the road as quickly as possible. Cold and tired as you are, you have new energy from the feeling that you're going to make it. The road is fairly steep, and your foot feels as if it's made of solid rock, but you make good progress. At last you reach the highway. For a long, cold twenty minutes you walk along the highway, looking both ways in the hope of seeing an on-coming car. Finally you see a truck coming along. You stand in the middle of the road and wave it down.

You tell the driver about the plane crash and your efforts to get help for Jake. "I think my foot may be frozen," you add.

"Lucky for you," the driver says, "there's a resident Mountie in Cartwright—that's a lumber camp about twenty miles down the road. They should be able to get a medic to you pretty quickly."

Go on to the next page.

An hour later you are sitting on a stool in the medical clinic in Cartwright. Your foot is thawing in a bucket of very warm water. It hurts—even with the painkillers you've taken—but you're smiling. The Mountie has just given you two great pieces of news: Your foot is going to be okay, and a helicopter team has safely lifted Jake off the mountain!

The End

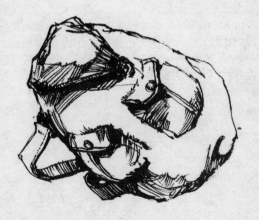

ABOUT THE AUTHOR

EDWARD PACKARD, a graduate of Princeton University and Columbia Law School, practiced law in New York and Connecticut before turning to writing full time. He developed the unique storytelling approach used in the Choose Your Own Adventure® series while thinking up stories for his children, Caroline, Andrea, and Wells.

ABOUT THE ILLUSTRATOR

LESLIE MORRILL is a designer and illustrator whose work has won him numerous awards. He has illustrated over thirty books for children, including the Bantam Classic edition of *The Wind in the Willows; Indian Trail,* a Bantam Skylark Choose Your Own Adventure® book; and *Lost on the Amazon,* a Choose Your Own Adventure® book. His work has also appeared frequently in *Cricket* magazine. A graduate of the Boston Museum School of Fine Arts, Mr. Morrill lives near Boston, Massachusetts.

CHOOSE YOUR OWN ADVENTURE

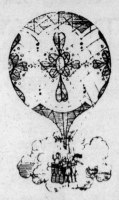

You'll want all the books in the exciting *Choose Your Own Adventure®* series offering you hundreds of fantasy adventures without ever leaving your chair. Each book takes you through an adventure—under the sea, in a space colony, on a volcanic island—in which you become the main character. What happens next in the story depends on the choices *you* make and *only you* can decide how the story ends!

☐	23186	MYSTERY OF THE MAYA #11 R. A. Montgomery	$1.95
☐	23175	INSIDE UFO 54-40 #12 Edward Packard	$1.95
☐	23332	THE ABOMINABLE SNOWMAN #13 R. A. Montgomery	$1.95
☐	23236	THE FORBIDDEN CASTLE #14 Edward Packard	$1.95
☐	22541	HOUSE OF DANGER #15 R. A. Montgomery	$1.95
☐	22768	SURVIVAL AT SEA #16 Edward Packard	$1.95
☐	23290	THE RACE FOREVER #17 Ray Montgomery	$1.95
☐	23292	UNDERGROUND KINGDOM #18 Edward Packard	$1.95
☐	23295	SECRET OF THE PYRAMIDS #19 R. Brightfield	$1.95
☐	23294	ESCAPE #20 R. A. Montgomery	$1.95
☐	23324	HYPERSPACE #21 Edward Packard	$1.95
☐	23349	SPACE PATROL #22 J. Goodman	$1.95
☐	23366	THE LOST TRIBE #23 L. Foley	$1.95
☐	23733	LOST ON THE AMAZON #24 R. A. Montgomery	$1.95
☐	23661	PRISONER OF THE ANT PEOPLE #25 R. A. Montgomery	$1.95
☐	23635	THE PHANTOM SUBMARINE #26 R. Brightfield	$1.95
☐	23868	MOUNTAIN SURVIVAL #28 Edward Packard	$1.95
☐	23867	THE HORROR OF HIGH RIDGE #27 Julius Goodman	$1.95

Prices and availability subject to change without notice.

Now you can have your favorite Choose Your Own Adventure® Series in a variety of sizes. Along with the popular pocket size, Bantam has introduced the Choose Your Own Adventure® series in a Skylark edition and also in Hardcover.

Now not only do you get to decide on how you want your adventures to end, you also get to decide on what size you'd like to collect them in.

SKYLARK EDITIONS

☐	15120	The Circus #1 E. Packard	$1.75
☐	15207	The Haunted House #2 R. A. Montgomery	$1.95
☐	15208	Sunken Treasure #3 E. Packard	$1.95
☐	15149	Your Very Own Robot #4 R. A. Montgomery	$1.75
☐	15308	Gorga, The Space Monster #5 E. Packard	$1.95
☐	15309	The Green Slime #6 S. Saunders	$1.95
☐	15195	Help! You're Shrinking #7 E. Packard	$1.95
☐	15201	Indian Trail #8 R. A. Montgomery	$1.95
☐	15191	The Genie In the Bottle #10 J. Razzi	$1.95
☐	15222	The Big Foot Mystery #11 L. Sonberg	$1.95
☐	15223	The Creature From Miller's Pond #12 S. Saunders	$1.95
☐	15226	Jungle Safari #13 E. Packard	$1.95
☐	15227	The Search for Champ #14 S. Gilligan	$1.95

HARDCOVER EDITIONS

☐	05018	Sunken Treasure E. Packard	$6.95
☐	05019	Your Very Own Robot R. A. Montgomery	$6.95
☐	05031	Gorga, The Space Monster #5 E. Packard	$7.95
☐	05032	Green Slime #6 S. Saunders	$7.95

Prices and availability subject to change without notice.

Buy them at your local bookstore or use this handy coupon for ordering:

Bantam Books, Inc., Dept. AVSH, 414 East Golf Road, Des Plaines, Ill. 60016

Please send me the books I have checked above. I am enclosing $_____ (please add $1.25 to cover postage and handling). Send check or money order—no cash or C.O.D.'s please.

Mr/Ms _____

Address _____

City/State _____ Zip _____

AVSH—1/84

Please allow four to six weeks for delivery. This offer expires 7/84.